Hey Jack! Books

First American Edition 2015
Kane Miller, A Division of EDC Publishing

Text copyright © 2014 Sally Rippin
Illustration copyright © 2014 Stephanie Spartels
First published in Australia in 2014 by Hardie Grant Egmont

For information contact:
Kane Miller, A Division of EDC Publishing
P.O. Box 470663
Tulsa, OK 74147-0663
www.kanemiller.com
www.edcpub.com
www.usbornebooksandmore.com

Library of Congress Control Number: 2014950306

Printed and bound in the United States of America
2 3 4 5 6 7 8 9 10

ISBN: 978-1-61067-393-8

The Big Adventure

By Sally Rippin

Illustrated by Stephanie Spartels

Kane Miller
A DIVISION OF EDC PUBLISHING

Big smile

sleeping bag

favorite boots

Happy Mood

Chapter One

This is Jack. Today Jack
is in a happy mood.
It's school vacation and
he is going camping
with his family!

Jack's parents pack the car. It is **stuffed** to the very top.

"Have we got everything?" his dad asks.

"I think so," says his mom.

"What about the marshmallows?" Jack asks.

"Yes." Jack's mom smiles.

"Don't worry. I wouldn't forget the marshmallows."

3

Jack grins. Toasted marshmallows are his favorite camping treat!

They drive a long way until they reach the campsite. It is next to a beach.

Jack can hear the **roar** and **crash** of waves in the distance.

4

"Can we go for a swim?" he begs.

He can't wait to get into the water.

"Not just yet," his dad says. "We have to put up the tent first."

Jack helps his mom and dad put up the tent.

It is very hard work.

And Scraps definitely

isn't helping!

Jack's job is to hammer the pegs into the ground. Soon he is very hot and very sweaty.

Finally the tent is up. They sit in the shade and have a cool drink.

"Can we go to the beach now?" asks Jack. "Please?"

"Yes!" Jack's dad says.
"Put your bathing suit on.
I'll grab the towels."

Soon everyone is ready.
They walk along a path
that winds through the
scrub.

Jack chases Scraps up a
sand dune. When he sees
the sea, he cheers.

He can't wait to jump
into the cool blue water.

Jack and his dad splash in the waves while his mom reads a book. They throw a tennis ball for Scraps.

"He's a good swimmer, isn't he?" Jack says.

"He sure is," Jack's dad says. "OK, time to get out now."

"Aw, can't I stay in a bit longer?" Jack asks.

"No, Jack," his dad says. "The current here is very strong.

"It's dangerous to go in the water without an adult, OK?" his dad adds.

"OK," sighs Jack.

They **trudge** up the sand to get dry. Jack's dad lies on his towel and closes his eyes. Jack's mom is dozing too.

How boring! Jack thinks.

How can they sleep
when there is a whole
beach to explore?

Chapter Two

"Can I go for a walk
with Scraps?" Jack asks.

"Hmm, I don't know,"
Jack's mom says. "I'd
rather you stayed here."

"I'm not a little kid anymore, Mom!" Jack says. "And I'll have Scraps with me."

"All right, but don't go farther than the tide pools," she says.

"And don't go into the water," his dad mumbles **sleepily**.

"I won't," says Jack.

Jack wanders along the beach picking up shells. Scraps chases seagulls.

Soon they reach the tide pools. They are full of interesting things. Jack sees spiky black mussels, little brown crabs and even an orange starfish.

But then, in the distance, Jack sees something even more interesting. A small dark cave in the cliff.

Jack turns to look at his parents. They are still sleeping.

The cave isn't much farther than the tide pools, he thinks. *I'm sure it's OK if I just take a quick peek.*

Jack and Scraps run up to the cave. Inside it is very cool and very quiet. The sea sounds a million miles away.

"Wow! Isn't this great?"
Jack says to Scraps.

Scraps barks and the
echo barks back at him.
He **whimpers** and
hides behind Jack's legs.

"I thought you were
braver than that!" Jack
giggles. "Hey, let's
pretend we're cavemen.

20

This can be our house."

Jack looks around for things to decorate their cave. He makes a bed out of a big piece of seaweed. Then he finds some shells they can use as bowls. He collects bits of wood to make a pretend fire.

"Doesn't it look great, Scraps?" he says. "I wish we could stay here forever!"

Jack pretends he is "Grunt, the caveman." Scraps is his ferocious pet wolf. Though he doesn't look very ferocious right now!

Jack and Scraps play cavemen for a little while.

"Come on, Scraps!" Jack says. "We'd better go back. Mom and Dad might be worried."

Scraps runs to the entrance of the cave, then stops. Jack stops too.

24

A little while ago there was sand in front of the cave. Now there is water.

Deep, splashing water. The tide has come in.

Jack and Scraps are trapped!

Chapter Three

Jack feels very frightened.

"Dad!" he calls loudly.
"Mom!"

"Dad! Mom!" the echo
calls back.

Jack knows they will never hear him. They are too far away. And the sea is much too **loud**.

Jack swallows back his tears. *What if no one ever finds us?* he worries. *It will be dark soon!*

Jack wishes he had never left the tide pools.

He wishes he had stayed with his mom and dad.

Just then, Scraps' ears stand up. He tilts his head to one side and begins to bark. The echo joins in.

"What is it, Scraps? Can you hear Mom and Dad?" Jack asks.

He tries to listen more carefully. But all he can hear is Scraps barking and the roar of the waves.

Scraps runs along the edge of the water.
He barks and barks.

Jack **yells** as loudly as he can. But he knows it's no use. If he can't hear his parents they won't be able to hear him. Only Scraps has hearing like a superhero.

Maybe I should try and swim out to them? he thinks. *No. Dad said I can't go into the water without him.*

But then Jack has an idea. His dad said that *he* shouldn't go into the water. But he didn't say *Scraps* shouldn't go into the water.

"Scraps!" he says. "Go find Dad! Please, little buddy! Go find Mom and Dad!"

Scraps looks at Jack.

Then he leaps into
the water.

The waves are very
strong. But Scraps
paddles fiercely.

Soon he disappears behind a big rock.

"Go, Scraps!" Jack yells. He crosses his fingers tightly on both hands. He holds his breath and his heart beats fast.

Just then, Jack sees someone wading towards him.

34

Next to him swims a
very brave puppy.

"Dad!" Jack yells. "Scraps!"

He bursts into tears.

"I was so scared."

Jack's dad takes Jack in his arms. "We were scared too," he says **angrily**. "We looked for you everywhere. You should never have come this far without us!"

Jack hangs his head.

"I know," he says. Big tears
slide down his nose and
drop onto the ground.

"It's OK," Jack's dad says. "I know you've learned your lesson. The main thing is that we found you!"

"Thanks to Scraps," Jack says, hugging his dog. "You are the **bravest** dog in the world!"

38

"And you were good not
to go into the water, like
I told you," Jack's dad
says. "It's not very deep,
but the current is strong."

He lifts Jack up onto his shoulders. "Let's get back before it gets any deeper. I think it's time to go back to the campsite now."

40

That evening Jack sits
around the campfire
with his mom and dad,
toasting marshmallows.
Scraps lies at his feet.
He feels warm and
happy and cozy.

It's fun to be an adventurous explorer during the day, thinks Jack. *But at night, I prefer to just be a kid.*

Collect them all!